Zoe stepped closer. A little
round face peered sleepily over
the top of the crate. The animal
had brown fur with big black
patches around its eyes and its
mouth was curled into a smile.
"It's a sloth!" cried Zoe.

Look out for:

The Lonely Lion Cub

The Puzzled Penguin

The Playful Panda

The Silky Seal Pup

The Eager Elephant

The Lucky Snow Leopard

The Pesky Polar Bear

The Cuddly Koala

The Wild Wolf Pup

The Happy Hippo

The Sleepy Snowy Owl

The Scruffy Sea Otter

The Picky Puffin

The Giggly Giraffe

The Curious Kangaroo

Zoe's Rescue ZOO

The Super Sloth

Amelia Cobb

Illustrated by
Sophy Williams

nosy
crow

With special thanks to Siobhan Curham

For Sammie and Edi Venn

First published in the UK in 2018 by Nosy Crow Ltd
The Crow's Nest, 14 Baden Place
Crosby Row, London SE1 1YW

Nosy Crow and associated logos are trademarks and/or
registered trademarks of Nosy Crow Ltd

Text copyright © Hothouse Fiction, 2018
Illustrations © Sophy Williams, 2018

The right of Hothouse Fiction and Sophy Williams to be identified as the author
and illustrator respectively of this work has been asserted by them in accordance
with the Copyright, Designs and Patents Act 1988.

A CIP catalogue record for this book will be available from the British Library

Printed and bound in Great Britain by Clays Ltd, Elcograf S.p.A.

Papers used by Nosy Crow are made from wood grown in sustainable forests.

ISBN: 978 1 78800 150 2

www.nosycrow.com

Chapter One
The Rainforest Dome

Zoe Parker raced along the red-brick path through the Rescue Zoo as fast as her legs could carry her. Meep, a tiny mouse lemur, scampered beside her, his long tail bobbing up and down. As they ran past the penguin enclosure two of the penguins waddled out of the water to greet them, their black feathers shiny and wet.

"Hello, Pip! Hello, Percy!" called Zoe. "Sorry we can't stop and chat but we're very busy."

"Busy, busy, busy!" agreed Meep.

Zoe giggled and picked the little lemur up and placed him on her shoulder. "There you are, Meep. It'll be quicker if I carry you!"

Zoe had a very special secret. On her sixth birthday she had realised that she could talk to the animals! She could understand every word they said, and they understood her. No one else knew, not even Zoe's mum or Great-Uncle Horace. Zoe was always careful not to chat to her animal friends when anyone else was close by.

A cool breeze suddenly blew up the path and Meep snuggled closer to Zoe.

"Don't worry," said Zoe. "You'll soon be nice and warm."

Up ahead, some visitors to the zoo were gathered in front of the giraffe enclosure, watching as Jewel and her son Jamie trotted down to the stream for a drink of water. But Zoe didn't have time to stop and say hello.

Zoe wasn't a visitor to the zoo. She lived there in a cottage with her mum Lucy, who was the zoo vet. Meep lived with them too. The Rescue Zoo had been started by Zoe's Great-Uncle Horace, who was a world-famous explorer and animal expert. He'd created the zoo as a safe place for animals to live if they were lost, hurt or endangered.

As the path wound away from the giraffe enclosure, a huge glass dome came into view in the field at the back of the zoo. It looked like a giant bowl that had been placed upside down on the grass.

Zoe's heart pounded with excitement. The Rainforest Dome was the newest enclosure at the Rescue Zoo. It was going to be opening for visitors at the weekend in a special ceremony, and the zoo staff had been very busy getting the dome ready. For the past few weeks Zoe had spent every spare moment of her time helping them, rushing there each day after school.

As Zoe got closer to the dome, she could hear the faint squawks of the parakeets and the screeches and chattering of the monkeys inside. Meep hopped down from her shoulder and scampered over to the entrance.

He was just as excited as Zoe about the
new dome.

When Zoe got to the entrance she
felt for the silver pendant around her
neck. It was in the shape of a paw-print.

It had been a birthday present from Great-Uncle Horace and it opened the doors to all the enclosures. She pressed the silver charm to a panel and the dome door swung open. Meep raced inside and as Zoe followed him hot, steamy air wrapped around her. She took off her coat.

"It's so hot!" complained Meep.

"It has to be," replied Zoe. "It's so all the animals from the rainforest will feel at home." She heard a loud squawk and looked up. High above them, a couple of colourful parakeets were swooping in and out of the branches of the palm trees.

"Hello, Zoe, how was school?"

The cheerful voice came from the keeper's office. It was Valeria, the head keeper at the Rainforest Dome.

She looked after all of the animals who lived there. Valeria was wearing her uniform of Rescue Zoo T-shirt and shorts, and her long dark hair was tied back in a plait. Valeria was from Venezuela, a country in South America where they had real rainforests!

"Hi, Valeria. School was good, thanks," replied Zoe. "Have the tamarins arrived? Did the trumpeter birds settle in? Is there anything I can do to help?"

Valeria laughed. "Slow down, Zoe. One question at a time." She came over carrying a box of coconuts. "Yes, the emperor tamarin monkeys were moved from their old enclosure this morning. They're over in the trees on the other side of the stream." She pointed across the wide stream that ran through the centre

of the dome. Some monkeys were leaping through the top branches of the tall trees. Their fur was grey and black, apart from long white strands that drooped past their mouths like moustaches.

"They look like they're having a lot of fun," said Zoe as the monkeys chatted happily.

"They are," replied Valeria. "Tamarins are one of the friendliest species of monkeys in the world. They love to play." She smiled as one of the monkeys leapt on another's back. "And to answer your second question, the trumpeter birds have settled in really well. Their chick is nesting in the top of that palm tree." She pointed to one of the trees that had been planted next to the stream the day before. The mum and dad were strutting around on the ground beneath the tree looking for food. The feathers on their round bodies were mostly black, apart from splashes of shiny blue on their neck and wings.

The mum opened her large beak and let out a honking sound. Zoe grinned. She could see how they'd got their name. They really were as loud as trumpets! Great-Uncle Horace had told Zoe that some people in South America even used trumpeter birds to guard their houses because their warning cry was so noisy.

"And to answer your last question," continued Valeria. "Yes, there is something you can do to help me! We need to hang these coconuts from the trees for the monkeys." She took some coconuts from the box. They were attached to pieces of rope.

Zoe nodded and grinned. The monkeys loved chewing on coconuts to get to the sweet flesh inside.

"Can you hang some from the trees on this side of the stream and I'll do the other?" said Valeria.

"Of course." Zoe took the coconuts from her.

Valeria fetched a crate from the store room for Zoe to stand on so she could reach the branches, then Zoe took the rest of the coconuts over to the other side of the stream. As soon as Valeria had gone, Tammie the southern tamandua trundled past. When she saw Zoe, the little anteater made a snuffling noise to greet her.

"Hello, Tammie," smiled Zoe, crouching down to stroke her. Tammie was from Venezuela like Valeria. Her fur was brown, apart from the area around her chest, which was black and made her look as if she was wearing a vest. "Are you enjoying living in the Rainforest Dome?"

Tammie nodded and grunted.

Zoe smiled. "Good."

Like most of the other animals in the dome, Tammie had been moved there from another enclosure in the zoo. As Zoe hung a coconut from a branch she felt so happy. She couldn't wait until the dome's Grand Opening. There was less than a week to go now and most of the trees had been planted and most of the animals had arrived.

Just then Zoe heard the faint roaring of an engine coming from outside. Meep stood up straight, his ears pointing upright. A parakeet flying around the roof of the dome began to squawk with excitement. Soon all of the other birds were joining in and the monkeys shrieked and hooted.

The noise of the engine got louder. It sounded like a motorbike ... and Zoe could only think of one person who would ride their motorbike right into the Rescue Zoo. Great-Uncle Horace! But he was on a trip to Costa Rica and wasn't due back until the weekend.

Zoe raced over to the door with Meep scampering behind her and they hurried outside. It *was* Great-Uncle Horace! He was parking his motorbike on a patch of grass beside the dome. His helmet and motorbike were covered in stickers from all the exciting places he'd travelled to.

The air outside was filled with the sound of animals chirping, shrieking and roaring with excitement. They all loved it when Great-Uncle Horace came home. And so did Zoe!

A beautiful bright-blue bird fluttered from the sidecar of his bike and perched on the handlebars. It was Kiki, Great-Uncle Horace's hyacinth macaw. She went everywhere with him.

"Zoe! How are you?" called Great-Uncle Horace as he took off his goggles.

"Great-Uncle Horace!" Zoe exclaimed, running over to give him a big hug.

14

"What are you doing back so soon?"

"I have a new arrival for the dome," he replied. "She's from Costa Rica."

Just then Zoe's mum Lucy appeared, running up the path towards them. "Uncle Horace!" she cried, hugging him.

"He has a new animal for the Rainforest Dome," Zoe told her.

They both watched as Great-Uncle Horace took a crate from the sidecar and slowly opened the lid. "I'm not sure if she'll be awake," he said, peering inside. "This is one very sleepy little animal!"

Zoe stepped closer. What could it be?

A little round face peered sleepily over the top of the crate. Its fur was brown, with big black patches around its eyes and its mouth was curled into a smile.

"It's a sloth!" cried Zoe.

Chapter Two
A Sleepy Sloth

"A sloth indeed," replied Great-Uncle
Horace, lifting the animal from the crate.
"She's a three-toed sloth, to be precise."

"Three-toed?" echoed Zoe as she
stroked the sloth on top of her head. She
was quite small and her fur was really
soft. The sloth smiled up at Zoe sleepily.

"Yes," replied Great-Uncle Horace.

"There are two-toed sloths and three-toed sloths. Although, actually, all sloths have three toes."

Zoe looked at him, confused.

"They really should be called three-fingered, see." Great-Uncle Horace gently picked up one of the sloth's front paws. Three long claws curved out from it.

"Her claws are so long!" exclaimed Zoe.

"All the better for hanging from trees," he chuckled. "Do you want to hold her?"

"Yes, please!"

Great-Uncle Horace passed the sloth to Zoe. The sloth nestled her sleepy head against Zoe and closed her eyes. She was lovely and warm!

"She's around one year old," said Great-Uncle Horace as Kiki fluttered from the motorbike and perched on his shoulder. "Sadly, her mother was killed by hunters before she learned how to survive in the wild, so this little one will be a lot safer here with us."

"Poor thing," said Lucy sadly. "Still, she looks to be in good condition, thank goodness."

Zoe stroked the sloth's soft fur. She couldn't wait for them to be alone so she could talk to the zoo's newest member properly and find out more about her. Sloths were one of her favourite animals but she didn't really know much about them, apart from that they liked to sleep a lot!

The sloth opened her eyes again.

"She's probably hungry after our journey," said Great-Uncle Horace. "Let's go and get her something to eat."

Zoe smiled and they all went into the dome, with Meep scampering along beside them.

"What do sloths eat?" asked Zoe as they followed the path inside the dome.

"Well, when they're in the wild, they tend to eat leaves and plants," replied Great-Uncle Horace.

"But we can give her fruit and vegetables too," added Lucy.

The sloth slowly stretched out one paw.

"She looks so sleepy," said Zoe.

"Yes, sloths do need a lot of sleep," said Great-Uncle Horace. "They're actually one of the sleepiest of all the animals. They can sleep for fifteen to twenty hours a day."

"But that's nearly all day and all night!" exclaimed Zoe. She couldn't imagine sleeping for so long. She sat down on a bench by the stream so that the sloth could get a good look at her new home.

"Let's go and ask Valeria for some sloth snacks!" Great-Uncle Horace said to Lucy.

As soon as they'd gone Zoe cuddled the sloth closer to her. At last she could talk to the sloth and find out all about her!

"Hello, my name's Zoe," she whispered. "What's your name?" Meep hopped up on to the bench next to them and chattered hello.

The sloth gave some long squeaks. She spoke so slowly it took Zoe a while to understand what she was trying to say. "Your name is Sabina?"

The sloth slowly squeaked again.

"Welcome to the Rescue Zoo. I'm really sorry you lost your mum," said Zoe.

"But you'll be safe here and you'll make lots of new friends."

"Like me!" exclaimed Meep.

"Yes, and me," said Zoe.

Sabina smiled and looked around the dome.

"Do you like it in here?" asked Zoe. "It's just like the rainforest so hopefully you'll feel at home."

She watched the sloth carefully. She really hoped Sabina liked the dome.

Zoe knew all the visitors to the zoo would be super-excited to see a sloth! Sabina slowly nodded her head and gave another sleepy smile. Zoe sighed with relief.

Just then Great-Uncle Horace and Lucy came back with Valeria. The keeper was holding a plastic container of thinly sliced vegetables.

"Why don't you try feeding her some butternut squash?" she said, handing Zoe a thin slice.

Zoe held the butternut squash to Sabina's mouth and the little sloth began to nibble.

"Where do sloths sleep?" asked Zoe.

"In trees," replied Great-Uncle Horace. "Hanging from the branches, usually."

"They hang from branches even when they're fast asleep?" exclaimed Zoe.

"Don't they fall out?"

Great-Uncle Horace shook his head. "No, their extra-long claws grip to the branches and keep them safe."

Zoe smiled. Sloths were so cool! She couldn't wait until she was alone with Sabina again and could find out more about her.

All around the dome the animals chattered and chirped. It was getting dark outside now and twinkling spotlights had come on all around the dome. Once Sabina had finished the slice of butternut squash she gave a giant yawn.

"I think she's tired," said Zoe.

"Would you like to find her a tree to sleep in?" asked Valeria.

"Yes, please!" exclaimed Zoe.

They walked slowly down to the stream.

The trumpeter birds squawked a greeting from the top of their tree. There was another palm tree next to theirs, a little closer to the water.

"How about this one?" said Zoe. "It's got a lovely view of the stream."

Valeria nodded. "Yes, this looks like the perfect home."

Carefully, Zoe lifted the little sloth on to one of the lowest branches.

Slowly, using her claws to help her, Sabina clambered higher. Then, hanging from a branch by one arm, she closed her eyes and went to sleep.

Meep gazed up at her, his golden eyes wide.

Zoe heard footsteps behind them and turned to see Great-Uncle Horace and her mum.

"Look," whispered Zoe. "Sabina's already asleep."

"You do choose some lovely names for the animals, Zoe," said Lucy.

Zoe grinned. Of course, her mum didn't know that Sabina had *told* Zoe her name!

"I chose this tree for her," Zoe said to Great-Uncle Horace. "I thought it would be nice for her to be close to the water."

"Good work, Zoe!" replied Great-Uncle Horace, and Zoe beamed with pride. She wanted to be a zookeeper when she grew up so she loved helping the animals any way she could.

"Do you think she'll sleep for fifteen hours?" asked Zoe.

Lucy laughed. "Maybe! But, speaking of sleep, we'd better get back home before it gets too late. Don't forget you've got to work on your school project."

Zoe's class had been asked to study the plants and trees in their garden or local park and present their findings to the rest of the class. The trouble was, Zoe had been so busy helping get the Rainforest Dome ready that she hadn't even started her project! She wasn't too worried though, as she had till the end of the week to get it done.

Zoe whispered good night to Sabina, then scooped Meep into her arms and followed her mum and Great-Uncle Horace outside.

The sun had now set and the dome looked beautiful, lit up against the darkening sky. As they passed the giraffe enclosure Jewel stretched her long neck over the fence to say hello.

Zoe patted her on the head. "Good night, Jewel," she whispered.

When they got back to the cottage Zoe went straight to her bedroom to start work on her project while Lucy and Great-Uncle Horace made dinner. Zoe had borrowed Lucy's laptop to do some research on the plants that grew in her garden.

Zoe stared at the screen blankly. Looking at pictures of normal plants and flowers seemed a bit boring compared to being in the Rainforest Dome!

Meep sprung on to the door handle and up on to the peg on Zoe's door.

"Look, Zoe, I'm sleeping like a sloth,"

he called, shutting his
eyes and hanging
from the peg by
one paw.

Zoe giggled. "It
doesn't look very
comfortable."

"It isn't!" Meep
leapt down and
joined her on the bed.

"I'm glad I don't have to
sleep like a sloth," he said.

Zoe grinned and closed her mum's
laptop. She was a bit too tired to work
on her project tonight. She was glad she
didn't have to sleep like a sloth too … but
she was very happy one had come to live
at the zoo!

Chapter Three
A Busy Day

The next day Zoe woke up early, before the elephants trumpeted their cheery morning greeting. The first thing she thought about was the new dome. She wondered how Sabina had slept.

Zoe grinned as she remembered what Great-Uncle Horace had said about sloths sleeping for fifteen to twenty hours a day. The little sloth was probably still fast asleep!

"Wake up, Meep!" she said, gently nudging the little mouse lemur, who was also fast asleep at the foot of her bed.

"What is it? What's wrong?" said Meep, rubbing his eyes.

"Nothing's wrong. I just want to get up early so I can go and see Sabina before school. I want to find out more about sloths and what it's like to live in the real rainforest. Come on!" Zoe sprang up from the bed and began pulling on her school uniform.

"But I was having a lovely dream about a giant blueberry called Boo-Boo," grumbled Meep, closing his eyes again.

Zoe giggled. Even when he was asleep, Meep was always thinking about food!

"I promise I'll get you blueberries for breakfast," she said as she put on her shoes.

"Will one of them be called Boo-Boo?" asked Meep, opening one eye.

"Yes, we can call one of them Boo-Boo," smiled Zoe. "We can take them with us to the dome and you can have breakfast with the other animals."

"OK then." Meep opened his other eye and stretched. He hopped from the bed and scrambled on to Zoe's shoulder.

Downstairs in the kitchen Lucy was still in her dressing gown, filling up the kettle.

"Goodness, you're up very early," she said when she saw Zoe and Meep.

"Too early," Meep grumbled in Zoe's ear.

"Is it OK if I go to the dome before

school to see Sabina?" asked Zoe.

Lucy glanced at the clock on the wall. "OK, but don't stay too long. You don't want to be late for school."

"I won't. I'll take my breakfast with me and have it there." Zoe put some blueberries and bananas in a container, grabbed a carton of fruit juice from the fridge and headed for the door.

Outside, the spring sunshine was just starting to rise, making the leaves on the trees shiny green. The air was a bit chilly but Zoe was running way too fast to feel the cold.

"Morning, Shadow!" she called as she raced past the wolf enclosure.

Shadow, the grey wolf, barked a greeting.

"I can't stop and chat now," called Zoe.

"I'm in a bit of a rush. There's a new animal in the Rainforest Dome to get to know. A sloth called Sabina!"

Shadow yelped.

"Thanks, Shadow. I'll tell her you said hello," replied Zoe.

Next, she raced past the sea otter enclosure, where Sasha and her brothers and sisters were playing. When they saw Zoe and Meep they squeaked a greeting.

"Morning! Can't stop, I'm in a rush," cried Zoe.

"Ever since they built the dome you're always in a rush," said Meep, wrapping his furry arms tightly around her neck. "Rush, rush, rush, rush!"

Zoe laughed. "That's because there's been so much to do to get it ready. Don't worry, it'll quieten down once it's opened."

When they got to the dome, Zoe used her paw-print pendant to open the door. It was so early, Valeria wasn't even there yet. Zoe breathed in the warm air and took off her coat. Tammie the tamandua trundled up to Zoe and snuffled around her legs.

"Are you hungry?" Zoe asked the little anteater.

"*I'm* hungry!" squeaked Meep.

"You're always hungry!" laughed Zoe, peeling one of the bananas and handing it to him. Then she turned back to Tammie. "I'll get you some food as soon as Valeria gets here," she said. "I just need to check on Sabina first."

Zoe headed over to the stream and looked up into the palm tree where she'd left her, but Sabina wasn't there.

Zoe frowned. She'd thought the little sloth would still be fast asleep! Where could she be? She walked alongside the stream, looking up into the trees. High in the branches, a bright-green toucan squawked and the trumpeter birds fluffed up their feathers, but there was still no sign of the little sloth.

A marmoset monkey scampered by, chattering to itself excitedly. Zoe watched as it ran to the end of the bank. Then she saw why it was so excited. At the far end of the stream Sabina was slowly making her way up a tree trunk, with a baby marmoset clinging to her back!

"Look, Meep," she cried, pointing to the funny sight.

Meep looked up from his banana and grinned. But before Zoe could go over and chat to Sabina, Valeria arrived.

"Good morning, Zoe! You're here bright and early!"

"I wanted to check on Sabina before I went to school," said Zoe. "Look, she's carrying a baby marmoset!"

Valeria smiled. "Ah yes, I've seen sloths do this in the rainforest before. They're very sociable creatures – when they're not asleep! Now, would

38

you like to help me peel some vegetables for the animals' breakfast?" continued Valeria.

"Yes, please!" Zoe followed Valeria into the keeper's office.

Valeria took some carrots from a fridge in the corner and handed them to Zoe with a vegetable peeler. Valeria started preparing some leafy vegetables and Meep sat in the corner munching on his blueberries. Zoe began to peel the carrots. She hoped she'd have time to feed Sabina before she had to go to school.

Once the carrots were ready Zoe took one of them back to the stream, looking for Sabina. The little sloth was now curled up on the floor next to a bush, fast asleep.

"That's funny," Zoe said to Meep. "I thought sloths only slept in trees."

"Maybe she got arm-ache from all that hanging," suggested Meep.

Zoe wished Sabina was still awake. She would have loved to have fed her breakfast and found out how her first night had been.

"Zoe, it's time to go!"

Zoe turned to see Lucy heading into the dome, carrying her school bag.

"OK, Mum," Zoe called back. "See you later, Sabina," she whispered to the sleeping sloth, leaving the carrot on the ground next to her.

By the time Zoe got to school she felt really tired. She sat down at the table with her friends Nicola and Jack and put her hand over her mouth to hide a yawn. The first lesson of the day was science.

"I hope your projects are all coming along well," said Miss Hawkins as she handed out their science books. "Don't forget there's only a few days left before they're due in."

Zoe's heart sank. She still hadn't started her project!

"I've almost finished my project," said Jack. "I've made a chart of all the plants growing in the park."

"I've taken photos of the flowers in my back garden and made them into a collage," said Nicola.

Zoe's heart sank even further. Her friends' projects sounded great. She wished she'd almost finished hers too, but with all the work getting the Rainforest Dome ready she just hadn't had the time.

Miss Hawkins drew a flower on the whiteboard, beneath a bright-yellow sun. "Today we're going to look at how plants provide us with oxygen," she said. "And why do we need oxygen?"

Jack put up his hand.

"Yes, Jack?"

"To breathe?"

"That's right." Miss Hawkins smiled at him. "If it weren't for plants we would run out of oxygen to breathe."

As Miss Hawkins started talking about oxygen, Zoe's mind drifted back to the Rescue Zoo and all of the cool plants in the dome. She couldn't wait to talk to Sabina again and find out more about the real rainforest. She wondered if Sabina was still asleep.

At break time she told Nicola and Jack

all about the latest arrival to the zoo.

"I wish I could be a sloth and sleep all the time," said Jack.

"I wish I was able to sleep hanging from a tree!" Nicola grinned. "I can't wait till we can come and see the Rainforest Dome."

"I can't wait for you to see it too," replied Zoe, grinning as she thought about the Grand Opening. The mayor was coming to officially open the Rainforest Dome, and a photographer and a journalist from the local paper would be there too. It was going to be so much fun!

Chapter Four
Sabina's Strange Sleep

As soon as the bell rang for home-time, Zoe raced from the classroom and out into the playground. Lucy was waiting for her by the gate, holding two bags of shopping.

"Hi, Mum. Have you been to the dome today? Is it nearly ready for the Grand Opening? Did you see Sabina?"

"Whoa, slow down, Zoe!" laughed Lucy. "How was school?"

"OK. Can I go to the dome when we get back? I want to see if Sabina's awake."

"What about your school project?" asked Lucy. "There's only a couple of days left to do it."

"I know. I'll work on it after tea, I promise."

As they set off back home Lucy started chatting to one of the other mums, so Zoe raced on ahead. She really hoped Sabina would be awake. She couldn't wait to see her!

As usual, Meep was waiting for her when she got to the zoo, perched on the carving of a hot-air balloon on top of the huge gates. The balloon looked like the real hot-air balloon that belonged to Great-Uncle Horace. Along with his motorbike it was one of his favourite ways to travel the world!

"Hello, Meep," Zoe whispered to the little lemur. Zoe called back to Lucy, who was still chatting with one of the other mums. "I'm just going to go to the dome."

"OK, but don't be too long," replied Lucy.

"Look, Zoe," chattered Meep as he scampered along the gate and hung upside down from the carving of a branch. "Guess who I'm pretending to be."

But Zoe had already hurried through the gates and into the zoo. She wanted to get to the dome as soon as possible. She had to try and catch Sabina while she was awake. There were so many things she wanted to ask her!

"Zoe!" called Meep as he scampered along the footpath after her. "You didn't see who I was pretending to be."

"Sorry, Meep," replied Zoe. "I just really want to get to the dome to have a proper chat with Sabina." Zoe raced around the corner of the café at top speed ... and bumped straight into Mr Pinch, almost knocking him over! Her heart sank. Mr Pinch was the manager of the Rescue Zoo and he was usually in a bad mood.

"What is going on?" Mr Pinch frowned down at Zoe. "Is the zoo on fire?"

Zoe shook her head.

"Has an alien spaceship landed on the gift shop?"

Zoe giggled. "No."

"Then why the big rush?"

"I need to get to the Rainforest Dome

to see Sabina."

Mr Pinch sighed. "And who, might I ask, is Sabina?"

"She's a sloth. Great-Uncle Horace rescued her from Costa Rica. She's really cute but the trouble is, she's not awake very often. Sloths need fifteen to twenty hours sleep *every day*," explained Zoe.

"If you ask me, that makes her a bit lazy." Mr Pinch frowned. "Well, no running, please. This is a zoo, not a racetrack."

"Sorry, Mr Pinch." Zoe picked Meep up and carried on along the path, walking as fast as her legs could go.

When she got to the dome she pressed her silver paw-print pendant to the panel by the door and stepped inside. The air in the dome was hot and steamy as usual.

But Zoe felt a bit shivery, so she kept her coat on.

"Hi, Zoe!" called Valeria. She was standing by the hollowed tree stump where Tammie slept. "Come and take a look at this."

Zoe hurried over. Sabina was curled on the floor next to the tree stump, fast asleep.

"What's she doing there?" asked Zoe. "She went to sleep on the ground by a bush this morning. I thought sloths always slept in trees."

"I don't know." Valeria shrugged. "I found her there just now."

Zoe peered inside the hollow tree stump. Tammie was sitting inside, munching on a carrot. When she saw Zoe she snuffled hello.

"I can't believe she's asleep again,"

said Zoe, looking at Sabina with a sigh.
She loved getting to know all the animals
in the zoo, but it was going to be hard to
get to know Sabina if she was asleep all
the time!

"Never mind," said Valeria. "I have a fun
job you can help me with."

Zoe grinned at her excitedly. "What is
it?"

"I need to turn on the mist."

While Meep scampered off to play with
the monkeys, Zoe followed Valeria into
the keeper's office.

Valeria showed Zoe a monitor. "This
records the temperature and humidity
levels inside the dome," she explained.

"What does humidity mean?" asked
Zoe.

"It means the amount of water in the

atmosphere," explained Valeria. "There is a lot of water in the atmosphere in the rainforest, so we need to recreate it in our dome with the sprinklers." She showed Zoe which button to press, then they went back into the dome. Plumes of mist were coming through the sprinklers in the roof, filling the dome with steam.

"Wow, that's so cool!" exclaimed Zoe, then on the other side of the stream she spotted some men digging holes by the trees.

"What are they doing?" asked Zoe.

"They are planting lianas," replied Valeria. "Lianas are tropical vines that grow around trees. Eventually they will grow right to the top of the trees and make bridges between them for the monkeys to run across."

Zoe smiled as she pictured the monkeys
running across bridges of vines. It sounded
like a lot of fun!

While Valeria went back to the office,
Zoe walked over to the stream with Meep
close behind her. She looked up into the
palm tree where the trumpeter chick was

nesting. Its mum and dad were foraging
on the floor for some food. When they
saw Zoe they bellowed a greeting.

"Lovely to see you too," replied Zoe,
her ears ringing. Trumpeters were the
loudest birds she'd ever heard!

Zoe went back over to Tammie's tree

house. Sabina was still on the floor and looked like she'd just woken up. She didn't look very comfortable!

Zoe remembered what Great-Uncle Horace had said about sloths not being able to move well on the ground. "I'll put you back in your nice tree," she smiled, picking Sabina up.

The little sloth gave a loud, slow squeak. She spoke so slowly and sleepily it was hard for Zoe to understand!

"Do you want something to eat?" asked Zoe, placing her carefully in the palm tree. "I can go and get you something if you like."

Sabina gave another squeak.

"What's she saying?" asked Meep.

"I'm not sure." Zoe frowned. "It sounds like 'day'." She stroked Sabina. "Yes, it's daytime. I'll go and get you some food!"

Zoe raced over to the office and grabbed a couple of peeled carrots from the fridge. Then she raced back to the palm tree.

Sabina was now hanging upside down from the branch. Zoe stood beneath her and held the carrot up to Sabina's mouth.

Sabina smiled and slowly squeaked.

"What's she saying?" asked Meep.

"I'm not sure," replied Zoe. "Something beginning with y."

"Yellow?" suggested Meep. "Yes? Yawn?"

Zoe listened more carefully. "No, she's saying yum." She gave Sabina some more carrot.

"Yum yum yum!" chattered Meep, jumping up and down. "When's it time for my tea, Zoe?"

"Soon," replied Zoe. "Here, have this as a snack for now." She handed Meep the other carrot.

Meep held the carrot in his front paws and took a big bite. "I wish I could eat upside down like Sabina."

"I think you might get tummy ache if you did," grinned Zoe.

Just as Sabina finished her carrot, Lucy came into the dome. "Tea's ready, Zoe," she called.

"OK, Mum." Zoe stroked Sabina on the head. "I'll come and see you again tomorrow," she whispered in the sloth's ear.

Sabina gave her a sleepy smile.

Zoe picked up Meep and went over to join her mum.

It was only when they got back to the cottage that she realised she hadn't asked Sabina what she was doing sleeping on the floor instead of her tree. She'd just have to ask her tomorrow.

Chapter Five
Sneezes and School

The next day when Zoe woke up, she felt really cold, even though she was wearing her fleecy zebra pyjamas. Her throat felt scratchy and dry too. *I hope I'm not getting poorly*, she thought to herself as she sat up in bed. She couldn't get ill this week – not when it was the opening of the dome!

"Morning, Zoe!" chattered Meep as he leapt up from his cushion at the end of the bed.

"Morning ... *atishoo!*" Zoe sneezed loudly.

"My name isn't Atishoo!" chirped Meep.

"I know," Zoe sniffed. "I was sneezing. Come on, let's get up and go to the dome." Hopefully, if Sabina was awake she'd get a chance to have a proper chat to her this time. And she could help to feed all the other rainforest creatures too. She quickly put on her school uniform and went downstairs.

"Morning, love," said Lucy as Zoe went into the kitchen. "Would you like some toast?"

"Yes, please. But would it be OK to take it to the dome?"

"I don't know." Lucy frowned. "You're looking a bit pale. I think you might have been overdoing it recently. Have a proper breakfast here this morning and go to the dome after school."

"But…" Zoe felt a tingling in her nose. "*Atishoo!*"

"Oh dear. I hope you're not coming down with a cold." Lucy popped some bread in the toaster and placed a bowl of berries on the table for Meep.

"I'm not. It was just a sneeze," said Zoe, but the scratchy feeling in her throat was getting worse.

"You can see Sabina and the other animals in the dome *after* school," said Lucy firmly, pouring her a glass of juice.

Zoe sat down at the table and sighed. She wanted to find out why Sabina had been sleeping by Tammie's tree stump, and what the rainforest was like in Costa Rica, and what she thought of the dome … and so many other things!

"So how are you getting on with your project, Zoe?" Miss Hawkins asked later, as the class were about to go for lunch.

"OK," replied Zoe.

"What kind of plants are you doing it on?"

"Oh – er – I haven't quite decided yet," stammered Zoe.

Miss Hawkins frowned. "But it's due in on Friday."

"I know. I'm starting it tonight."

Miss Hawkins nodded. But she looked disappointed. Zoe felt a horrible churning feeling in her tummy. She'd never been late with her school work before but she'd been so excited helping out with the Rainforest Dome. This evening she would do loads of work on her project. She didn't want to let Miss Hawkins down!

By the time home-time came around Zoe felt really shivery and tired and her throat was starting to hurt.

"Are you all right, love? You're very quiet," said Lucy as they made their way along the road.

"Yes, I'm fine," said Zoe. She didn't want to tell her mum she was feeling poorly or she wouldn't let her go and see Sabina!

"Hmm, you don't look great," replied Lucy. "You can spend twenty minutes at the dome but then you have to come home and finish your project. And then it's an early night for you!"

Zoe gulped. She hadn't even *started* her project, although she had come up with an idea, at least – she'd decided to make a model of some plants growing in the cottage garden. "OK. Thanks, Mum."

As soon as they got back to the zoo, Zoe set off for the dome with Meep. This time the little mouse lemur raced ahead. Zoe felt too tired to run.

When they got to the dome she went straight over to the palm trees by the stream. The trumpeter birds were perched at the top of theirs, feeding their fluffy chick. Sabina was tucked up on a branch below them, fast asleep.

"Look," said Zoe, picking Meep up so he could see. "Sabina's in a different tree."

Just then Valeria came over. "Hi, Zoe.

I was wondering if you could do something for me?"

"Of course," replied Zoe.

"We need some more bunting for the Grand Opening on Saturday. Could you go over to the gift shop and get some for me?"

"Of course. *Atishoo!*" Zoe sneezed.

"Oh dear, I hope you're not coming down with something," said Valeria.

Sabina stirred on her branch and opened her eyes.

"My sneeze woke her up!" exclaimed Zoe.

Sabina gave her a sleepy smile.

"Why don't you take Sabina with you to the shop," suggested Valeria.

"Really?" Zoe's eyes lit up.

"Yes, it will be a treat for her to see the

rest of the zoo," smiled Valeria. "I'll fetch
you a blanket to wrap around her so she
keeps nice and warm."

As Valeria went to
fetch a blanket, Zoe
carefully lifted
Sabina from the
branch and held
her tightly in her
arms. Then she
crouched down
so that Meep
could hop on to her
shoulder.

A few moments later,
with Sabina snuggled in Zoe's arms,
the three friends set off to the gift shop.
Outside the dome the evening sun was
shining and the trees lining the path

swayed in the breeze.

Zoe hurried along the path towards the lion enclosure. She wanted Sabina to get to see as much of the zoo as possible, but she didn't have much time before she had to go home to work on her project!

Sabina slowly started squeaking a word.

"T-r-e-e," echoed Zoe. "Tree! Yes, there are lots of trees here in the zoo. You'll have to tell me all about the trees you have in the rainforest."

Sabina squeaked some more.

"Palm tree?" Zoe hurried on down the path.

Sabina gave a really loud squeak.

"What's scary?" asked Zoe. Then she realised that they were walking right by the lion enclosure. Leonard the largest lion was sitting by a rock in the middle of the enclosure. When he saw them, he tipped his head back and gave a big roar.

"Oh, you don't have to be scared of *these* lions. They're really friendly." She hugged Sabina tighter to her and walked over to the fence.

"Hello, Leonard," Zoe called back to him. "This is Sabina. She's a sloth from Costa Rica."

Leonard roared again. "He says welcome to the zoo," Zoe explained to Sabina.

Sabina smiled and slowly squeaked. "He's … very…"

Zoe tried to wait patiently for Sabina to finish her sentence. But it took such a long time! "Yes, he is very big," she interrupted. "One of the biggest cats in the zoo! I know, let's go and see the seals." She hurried off along the path towards the seal enclosure. If they were lucky they'd get there for feeding time.

Sure enough, Lorna the seal keeper was standing at the edge of the pool, holding a bucket of fish. "Seals are very clever," Zoe said to Sabina. "They catch their food in their mouths – look."

Lorna threw a fish into the air. One of the seals leapt out of the water and caught it in its mouth.

Sabina's smile grew bigger and her dark eyes shone with excitement.

Zoe felt another sneeze tingling in her nose.

"*Atishoo!*"

Meep jumped down from her shoulder in fright.

"Sorry, Meep. I think I must have caught a cold," said Zoe sadly.

"How do you catch a cold?" asked Meep. "Do you catch it in your mouth like seals catch fish?"

Zoe laughed. "Not exactly. Come on, we'd better hurry up and get to the shop."

By the time Zoe got to the gift shop she was so shivery her teeth were chattering.

Sally, the manager of the gift shop, was tidying the cuddly toy animals.

"Aha, there you are!" she said when she saw Zoe. "Valeria called and told me you were bringing a special visitor."

"This is Sabina," said Zoe.

Sally came over and Sabina gave her a sleepy smile.

"She's lovely!" exclaimed Sally. Then she looked at Zoe and frowned. "Are you all right, Zoe? You look very pale."

"I think I have a cold," sniffed Zoe. Sally patted her on the shoulder. "Best place for you is tucked up in bed."

As Sally went off to get the bunting, Zoe's heart sank. She really didn't want to be tucked up in bed. How would she get her project done? How would she be able to help at the dome? And what if she wasn't better in time for the Grand Opening?

Chapter Six
Mr Pinch and
the Project

By the time Zoe got back home she felt
so poorly she couldn't pretend to her
mum that there was nothing wrong.

"I don't feel very well," she said glumly
as she walked into the kitchen.

"Oh, you poor thing," said Lucy, giving
her a hug. "Go and get into bed and I'll
bring you a nice hot mug of soup."

"But there are so many things I need to do," said Zoe. "I need to do my school project. I was going to make a model of some plants. And I need to help at the Rainforest Dome and I need to—*Atishoo!*"

"You need to go to bed," said Lucy.

"But—"

"No buts," said Lucy firmly. "I'm sure if you get a good night's sleep you'll feel a lot better in the morning."

Zoe trudged up to her bedroom and got into her pyjamas.

"Can I be poorly too?" asked Meep, hopping on to the bed.

Zoe shook her head. "It's no fun being poorly," she said, snuggling under her duvet. She hoped her mum was right. She hoped she'd feel better in the morning.

When Zoe woke up the next day sunlight streamed into her bedroom through a gap in the curtains. She looked at the clock on the wall and frowned. It was way past her normal getting-up time.

"Oh no! I'm going to be late for school!" she exclaimed. "*A– atishoo!*"

"Eeek!" Meep jumped off the bed in fright. "Zoe! Your sneezes are scary!"

"Sorry, Meep." Zoe sat up in bed. Her throat was still sore and her nose was runny. She still wasn't feeling very well.

Lucy came into the room holding a tray. "Morning, love," she said. "How are you feeling?"

"Still a bit poorly," sniffed Zoe.

Her mum opened the curtains. "That's why I let you sleep in late. I've made you

some breakfast and I've called the school
to let them know you won't be in today."
Lucy put the tray on Zoe's bedside table.
On it was a glass of orange juice and a
bowl of porridge with some blueberries
sprinkled on top. There was also a bowl
of seeds and berries for Meep.

"But what about the model for my
project, and what about Sabina?"
said Zoe. "And I need to help get the
Rainforest Dome ready for Saturday."

"You need to rest and stay in the
warm," said Lucy. "Rushing about all
over the place will only make your cold
worse. I think you've tired yourself out
with all the time you've been spending in
the dome."

Zoe sighed. She hoped Sabina wouldn't
be worried when she didn't visit her. She'd

told her she'd come and see her again
today, and she still had so many questions
for the little sloth!

A little later that morning Lucy came
back into the bedroom. She was wearing
her vet's uniform and carrying her special
bag. A stethoscope was poking out of the
top.

"I have to pop to the zoo hospital," she said. "One of the big kangaroos has hurt its paw. How are you feeling?"

"A bit bored," replied Zoe.

"Why don't you put on your dressing gown and go and watch some TV in the living room?" said Lucy. "I won't be gone for long and maybe when I come back we can work on your project."

"OK." Zoe nodded. She wished she knew which plants she was going to make a model of. Thinking about it made her head hurt.

A few minutes later Zoe was enjoying an episode of her favourite TV show when there was a knock on the front door.

Meep hopped down from the back of the sofa. "Who is it, Zoe?"

"I don't know. Let's see." Zoe peeped through the window. Her heart sank. "It's Mr Pinch."

"Uh-oh!" exclaimed Meep.

Zoe opened the front door. "Hello, Mr Pinch. My mum isn't here. She had to go to the hospital to look after a kangaroo."

"I know. She asked me to come and see you," replied Mr Pinch.

"What? Why?" said Zoe in surprise.

"She's going to be a bit longer than she expected."

"Oh. OK. Thank you for letting me know," replied Zoe.

"And she told me you had a model to make, for your school project." Mr Pinch shifted from one foot to the other awkwardly. His polished shoes shone in the sunlight. "She said you might need some help."

"Yes, but…" Zoe was really shocked. Was Mr Pinch offering to help her?

Mr Pinch coughed. "It just so happens that I was an expert model-maker when I was a boy."

"Oh." Zoe looked at Meep, who was sitting totally still, staring up at Mr Pinch. He looked as shocked as Zoe felt.

"So if I can be of any assistance…" Mr Pinch looked at Zoe.

"That would be great," stammered Zoe. "Come in."

"So, where are your materials?" asked Mr Pinch as they went through to the living room.

"My what?"

"What materials are you using to make your model?"

"Oh – er – I'm not exactly sure."

Mr Pinch frowned. "Well, what is your model going to be?"

Zoe's face flushed. "I – I don't know."

Mr Pinch's frown grew. "You don't know?"

"No. Well, I'll probably make one of the plants in our garden."

"Hmm." Mr Pinch carried on frowning.

Zoe sighed. Working on her project would be no fun at all if Mr Pinch was going to be so grumpy about it!

"I can't seem to escape from plants at the moment," said Mr Pinch. "What with all the extra plants arriving every day for the Rainforest Dome."

Zoe suddenly felt a burst of excitement. "That's it!" she exclaimed. "I could make my model of the tropical plants in the

dome!" She looked at Mr Pinch. What
would he think of her idea?

For once, Mr Pinch didn't look grumpy.
In fact, he looked close to smiling.

"We need paper and a pen," he said.

"What for?"

"To make a list."

Zoe went
and fetched
her pens
and a
pad.

"OK,
what kind of plants are in the dome?"
asked Mr Pinch.

"There are palm trees," replied Zoe.
"And lily pads in the stream. And the
calabash trees that the monkeys play in.
Oh, and lianas."

"Right." Mr Pinch wrote down a list. "And you'll need something for the dome as well."

Zoe nodded. What could they use? "I know!" she exclaimed. "Mum has a big glass mixing bowl. If we turned it upside down it would look just like the dome."

"Excellent!" said Mr Pinch.

Zoe could hardly believe her ears. Mr Pinch had never praised her before.

"Now we need to collect our materials," said Mr Pinch.

Zoe went over to her arts and crafts cupboard and returned with some coloured card and tissue paper, pipe cleaners, glue and modelling clay.

First they made a base for the dome from cardboard, then Zoe drew a blue stream. Then she cut out some circles of pink tissue paper for the lily pads and stuck them on top of the water.

"What shall we use for the palm trees?" asked Mr Pinch.

"How about brown pipe cleaners for the trunks and the branches, and green card for the leaves?" suggested Zoe.

Mr Pinch nodded. "Good idea. I'll help you cut out the leaves when you've drawn them."

Zoe grinned. She couldn't believe Mr Pinch was being so nice!

By the time Lucy got home they had almost finished making the model dome. Zoe had gathered together some plastic animals to put inside the model.

"Goodness me, that looks amazing!" smiled Lucy. "Thank you so much for helping Zoe, Mr Pinch."

"Yes, thank you!" said Zoe.

Mr Pinch stood up. He looked a bit embarrassed. "Yes, well. I'd better be going now," he said. "This zoo won't run itself."

When he got to the door he stopped and turned back to Zoe. "Best of luck with your project," he said gruffly.

"Thank you, Mr Pinch."

Once he'd gone, Zoe looked at Lucy in shock. "He was so nice!"

"Yes, well, even Mr Pinch can be nice sometimes," said Lucy with a smile. "How are you feeling now?"

Zoe grinned. She'd been having so much fun making her model, she'd forgotten all about her cold. "Much better, thank you!"

Chapter Seven
A Special Visitor

The next day when Zoe woke up her sore throat had gone and her nose wasn't nearly as runny. She did feel really tired though. She put on her dressing gown and went down to see Lucy.

"I'm definitely a bit better," she told her mum as she came into the kitchen with Meep.

"Hmm." Lucy looked at her and put a hand on Zoe's forehead. "Well, you still look a bit pale and you're quite warm, so I think it's probably best if you stay home again today."

"But what about school? I need to hand my project in." Zoe looked at the model dome on the kitchen table.

"Don't worry. I'll call Miss Hawkins and tell her you'll bring it in on Monday."

"But what about Sabina? And the dome? It's the Grand Opening tomorrow and … *atishoo!*"

"And you want to be better for it so you need another day resting in the warm," said Lucy firmly.

"But I really miss Sabina," said Zoe.

Lucy put some toast on the table.

"Don't worry, you'll see her again soon," she said with a mysterious smile.

Later that morning Lucy went off to the zoo hospital to check on the poorly animals, and Zoe and Meep snuggled under a duvet on the sofa to watch TV. They'd only been watching for a few minutes when a voice boomed through the letter box.

"Hello! Is there anyone home?"

"Great-Uncle Horace!" cried Zoe, scrambling to her feet. She opened the door to see Great-Uncle Horace wearing a tweed jacket and holding a large picnic basket.

"How are you feeling today?" he asked.

"A lot better, thanks, but Mum said I should stay off school and rest till my cold has properly gone."

"Your mum is a very wise woman."
Great-Uncle Horace followed Zoe back
into the living room. "She told me you
might be in need of a special visitor."

"Yes. It's lovely to see you." Zoe sat back
down on the sofa and Meep hopped up
beside her.

"Oh, I wasn't talking about me!" Great-
Uncle Horace grinned and his eyes
twinkled. "No, I was talking about this
young lady." He placed the basket down
on the floor beside Zoe and lifted the lid.
Sabina was curled up inside it, fast asleep!

"Sabina!" exclaimed Zoe.

"Your mum thought that maybe you
could rest together," said Great-Uncle
Horace.

Zoe nodded eagerly.

"Valeria's prepared some snacks for her if she does wake up." Great-Uncle Horace handed Zoe a box of fruit and vegetables. "But until then I want you to be like a sloth and try to get some sleep." Great-Uncle Horace patted her on the head. "We need you to be well enough for the Grand Opening tomorrow."

Zoe nodded and snuggled beneath the duvet. Now Sabina was here, doing nothing didn't feel nearly as boring!

Great-Uncle Horace went into the kitchen and Zoe closed her eyes. In just a few moments she was fast asleep and dreaming about the Rainforest Dome. In her dream she was helping Valeria get everything ready for the Grand Opening but all of the animals had come down with colds and they wouldn't stop sneezing. She woke up suddenly to something touching her on the hand. She opened her eyes and saw Sabina's paw stretching out of the basket.

"Sabina! You're awake!" she whispered.

Sabina's smiling face appeared above the rim of the basket, before sinking back down. She looked so sleepy and cute.

"Aw, come here." Zoe leaned over and lifted Sabina on to the sofa with her.

Sabina gave two slow squeaks.

"No, you're not in the tree, you're in my house," replied Zoe.

Sabina let out some more slow squeaks about the tree but Zoe was too impatient to wait for her to finish her sentence. There was so much she wanted to say to the little sloth!

"Don't worry, we'll take you back soon.

Great-Uncle Horace brought you to see
me because I was feeling poorly. This is
our living room." She lifted Sabina up so
she could get a better view. "And there's
Meep." She pointed to the little lemur,
who was curled up asleep on a cushion
at the other end of the sofa. "We don't

normally sleep here. Normally we sleep in the bedroom. My mum lives here too but she's at work—"

Sabina suddenly squeaked again, much more loudly.

"Your tree?" Zoe frowned. Sabina certainly loved talking about her tree! "Yes, we'll take you back there soon."

Sabina gave another loud squeak but just then there were voices in the hallway and Great-Uncle Horace and Lucy came into the room.

"Aha, the patient is awake!" exclaimed Great-Uncle Horace.

"How are you feeling, love?" asked Lucy.

"Much better, thanks," replied Zoe, cuddling Sabina to her.

"I told you sleeping like a sloth would

do you the world of good," said Great-Uncle Horace.

Zoe grinned. He was right. She did feel a lot better.

"Would you like to give Sabina a snack?" asked Great-Uncle Horace.

Zoe nodded eagerly.

"I think we could all do with something to eat," said Lucy with a grin. As she and Great-Uncle Horace went into the kitchen to get some lunch ready, Zoe fetched the box of vegetables and took out a slice of butternut squash. Then she cradled Sabina in one arm and fed her with the other. The little sloth didn't seem that hungry though and kept squeaking loudly. At the other end of the sofa Meep opened his eyes. When he saw Zoe feeding Sabina he jumped up.

"Why are you having lunch without me?"

Zoe laughed. "Go through to the kitchen and Mum will get you something."

Once they'd all had lunch Great-Uncle Horace got to his feet.

"I suppose I should be getting Sabina back to the dome," he said.

"Can I take her?" asked Zoe. "Please! I'm feeling so much better now."

"OK, love," nodded Lucy. "Some fresh air would probably do you good. But you have to come straight back home."

"I will. I promise."

Zoe put Sabina in the basket and the little sloth went to sleep immediately. Then Zoe set off through the zoo, with Meep running along beside her.

The sun was shining and the sky was bright blue. Zoe was so happy to be outside again and to be feeling better. When she got to the dome she saw the new bunting hanging over the door. All the glass panels were shining brightly. Zoe's tummy tingled with excitement. Tomorrow the dome would finally be open to visitors! Using her paw-print pendant, she let herself in. Valeria was watering some of the new plants. "Hello, Zoe. How are you feeling?" she called.

"Much better, thanks."

"Did you enjoy your visitor?"

Zoe nodded. "Yes, thank you for letting her come and see me."

"You're very welcome. Would you like to put her back in her tree?"

"Of course." Zoe followed the path down to the stream. Lots of new plants had been planted right by Sabina's palm tree. It looked so bright and colourful.

"Look at the flowers," Zoe said to Sabina. She took her from the basket and held her up so she could see properly. "Aren't they beautiful?" But to her surprise, Sabina shook her head. The trumpeter birds flew down from their nest at the top of their tree and honked loudly.

"Hello!" said Zoe. "How's your chick?"

The trumpeter chick flapped its tiny wings and flew up out of its nest.

"Ah, look!" cried Zoe. "The chick's learned to fly!"

They watched as the chick flew in a circle, then made its way over to Sabina's tree and landed on one of the branches that hung over the stream.

"It's come to say hello!" exclaimed Zoe.

Sabina slowly stretched out her front paw, as if she was pointing at the tree.

"Yes, I know, the chick's up there," said Zoe.

Sabina gave a slow squeak but it was drowned out by the mummy trumpeter bird honking.

"That's great," replied Zoe. "I'm so pleased your chick likes her nest."

Sabina squeaked again. It sounded as if she was saying "not".

"Do you want me to put you up in the tree?" said Zoe. Before Sabina could answer, Zoe placed the little sloth on the same branch as the trumpeter chick.

Sabina let out another slow squeak.

"What did you say?" asked Zoe. But just then, Zoe saw Tammie trundling along the path towards her. She wondered if she needed feeding.

"Hey, Tammie, how are you? Are you hungry?"

Sabina slowly edged her way along the branch and gave another very loud squeak.

Zoe looked at her, puzzled.

Why did she keep
saying "not"?
High above she
heard a screech. She
looked up to see the
mummy marmoset
monkey scampering
through the tall trees
with her baby on her back.

As she got closer she leapt into the palm tree. There was a loud creaking sound.

Sabina squeaked loudly again.

"Not safe?" said Zoe. "What's not safe? Oh no!" She stared in horror as the palm tree started to tip forwards.

The trumpeter birds honked in alarm.

"The baby chick! Sabina!" Zoe gasped as the tree began to topple down towards the water.

Chapter Eight
The Super Sloth!

As the palm tree crashed towards the stream, the baby trumpeter chick went sailing through the air.

"Oh no!" gasped Zoe.

The trumpeter mum and dad honked loudly in alarm.

Out of the corner of Zoe's eye she caught a glimpse of brown fur falling, followed by a loud splash.

"Sabina!" cried Zoe as the little sloth fell into the water. Zoe knew that the stream was very deep in places. What was going to happen to Sabina and the chick?

Zoe ran to the very edge of the stream. Perhaps she could use a branch to fish

out the chick and Sabina? The baby trumpeter bird was flapping its wings, trying to stay afloat. Then Zoe saw Sabina swimming towards the chick. Zoe gasped. What was Sabina doing?

"Oh no!" exclaimed Zoe as the trumpeter chick disappeared beneath the water.

Sabina ducked under too, then reappeared a couple of seconds later.

"Look!" Zoe cried to Meep. "She's saved her!"

The little chick was now perched on Sabina's back, flapping the water from her wings.

Meep jumped up and down and the trumpeter mum and dad gave relieved hoots. Sabina began swimming back to the bank of the stream. She swam much slower this time, being careful not to drop the chick. When she got to the edge she slowly clambered on to the ground. The trumpeter birds hurried over to get their chick.

"Sabina, you're a hero!" exclaimed Zoe, picking up the wet sloth.

Sabina looked up at her and smiled.

"Is everything OK?" asked Valeria, running over. "I thought I heard you calling. Oh! What happened to the tree?"

"It crashed down," explained Zoe. "The trumpeter chick fell into the water. But Sabina saved it. She swam so fast!"

Valeria smiled. "That's amazing! Sloths are excellent swimmers. It's the only thing they can do fast." She bent down and had a look at the fallen tree. "I need to go and tell Mr Pinch what's happened," said Valeria. "Can you keep an eye on the animals for me?"

"Of course," replied Zoe.

When Valeria had gone Zoe gave Sabina a big cuddle. "You were so brave," she said.

Sabina squeaked.

Zoe waited patiently until she'd finished.

"Oh!" she gasped. "You knew that the tree wasn't safe all along as it was wobbly."

Sabina nodded and squeaked again.

"And you'd been trying to tell me." Zoe sighed. "I thought you were telling me how much you liked the tree! I'm really sorry I didn't listen properly."

Just then Tammie came over to see what was happening.

"Is that why I found you asleep on the ground by the bush and Tammie's tree stump?" remembered Zoe.

Sabina nodded.

The daddy trumpeter honked loudly, making Zoe, Meep and Sabina jump.

"He's right," cried Zoe. "Sabina, you're a superhero for saving their chick."

"Sabina the super sloth!" chattered Meep.

Tammie, the marmoset monkey and the trumpeter birds all snuffled and hooted and squawked in agreement.

Sabina grinned from ear to ear.

"What's all this noise about?"

Zoe turned to see Mr Pinch standing behind her.

"Er – the animals are just being happy," said Zoe quickly.

"Hmm, I don't see what they've got to be happy about." Mr Pinch frowned. "Not when we've got trees falling over the day before the Grand Opening!"

Zoe sighed. After being so nice and helping Zoe with her model, it seemed Mr Pinch was back to his grumpy old self again!

"Don't worry," said Valeria, coming over with two of the gardeners. "I'm sure we just need to dig a bigger hole for the tree. We'll soon fix it."

As the gardeners got to work replanting the palm tree, Zoe took Sabina to get a special treat.

"Here you go," said Zoe, feeding Sabina a slice of mango and hugging the sloth to her. "I'm really sorry I didn't understand you before. I promise I'll listen properly in future."

The little sloth squeaked happily and snuggled into Zoe.

The day of the Grand Opening was sunny and bright. Zoe woke up and smiled. Her throat didn't hurt, her nose wasn't runny and she hadn't sneezed all night. Her cold was gone!

"Wake up, Meep," she said, gently nudging the little lemur. "Today is the Grand Opening of the Rainforest Dome!"

"YAY!" cried Meep, leaping out of bed.

As soon as breakfast was over, Zoe and Meep got ready to set off for the Rainforest Dome. Just as they were about to leave there was a knock on the door.

"I think it might be for you," said Lucy with a mysterious smile on her face.

Zoe wondered who it could be. She opened the door to see Miss Hawkins standing there.

"Miss Hawkins!" she gasped.

"Hello, Zoe," replied Miss Hawkins. "How are you feeling?"

"Much better, thanks."

"I'm so glad to hear that," smiled Miss Hawkins. "Your mum asked me to call by on my way to the Grand Opening. She thought you'd like to show me your school project."

"Yes, I would!" exclaimed Zoe. She led Miss Hawkins through to the living room. She pointed to the model on the table. "I made a model of the Rainforest Dome."

"Zoe, that looks great," exclaimed Miss Hawkins as Zoe carefully lifted up the glass bowl so she could see inside.

Once Zoe had explained what the different plants were and how they were important to the different animals in

the Rainforest Dome, Lucy made Miss
Hawkins a cup of
tea and
Zoe and
Meep set
off for the
dome.

The zoo
was full
of noise. The
monkeys were
chattering, the elephants were trumpeting
and the penguins were squawking. As
Zoe walked past the giraffe enclosure she
smiled. Jamie and his mum Jewel were
trotting around happily, full of energy.
All of the animals knew something
very exciting was happening at the zoo
today!

The Super Sloth

On the lawn in front of the café, Mr Pinch was talking to the mayor and a journalist from the local paper, and a brass band were getting ready to play. The toot of the trumpets made Zoe think of the trumpeter chick. She still couldn't believe how brave Sabina had been. She really was a super sloth!

When they got to the dome Zoe saw that Valeria had hung strings of brightly coloured fairy lights around the entrance. It looked magical!

Zoe let herself in with her silver pendant. High above her a flock of parrots squawked a welcome. Zoe looked down to the bank of the stream. The palm tree was now totally upright again and Sabina was curled in one of the branches, fast asleep. Zoe smiled. She must have been very tired from all her swimming yesterday. She hoped Sabina would be awake for the opening ceremony!

After Zoe had helped Valeria feed the animals their breakfast she looked outside. A long queue of people was snaking along the path to the dome. She could see her friends Nicola and Jack at the front of the queue with their parents. Most of the rest of her class were there too – and Miss Hawkins. After missing school for two days Zoe was really happy to see her friends! Zoe went back over to the palm tree and the little sloth sleepily opened one eye.

"Yay, you're awake!" said Zoe. "It's almost time for the Grand Opening. Lots of people are here to see the dome."

Sabina slowly squeaked. This time Zoe

made sure she listened carefully until the sloth had finished her sentence.

"That's a lovely idea," smiled Zoe. Sabina had come up with a great idea for how to make the opening of the dome even more special.

"Ladies and gentlemen, boys and girls, monkeys, anteaters, parrots and sloths," Great-Uncle Horace boomed to the crowds of visitors gathered in front of the dome. "Welcome to the Rescue Zoo Rainforest Dome!"

The band played a trumpet fanfare as the mayor cut the ribbon tied around the entrance to the dome. The crowd cheered and burst into applause as they went into the dome, pointing at all the wonderful birds, animals and plants inside.

"This Rainforest Dome is a careful recreation of the rainforests in Central and South America," continued Great-Uncle Horace once everyone was inside the dome and gathered by the stream. "In here you will find the birds, animals, plants and trees that you would find in those rainforests."

Great-Uncle Horace gave the crowd a
big smile. "The Rainforest Dome is now
home to a very special three-toed sloth
from Costa Rica named Sabina."

He pointed to Sabina, who was
hanging from a branch of the palm tree.
"Now, most of you here probably
know that sloths are very sleepy animals!

But what you might *not* know is that they make excellent swimmers."

This was the moment Zoe had been waiting for. She nodded to Sabina and the little sloth dived from her branch down into the water. The crowd gasped.

"Oh no, the sloth's fallen in!" cried Nicola.

Zoe shook her head and grinned. "She's fine – look!"

Great-Uncle Horace let out a booming laugh as Sabina began swimming through the water. "Well, what perfect timing! She's giving you a demonstration."

The crowd gathered closer to the stream to get a better look. There was a loud cheeping sound and everyone gasped again as the trumpeter chick fluttered into the air and landed on Sabina's back!

"Wow!" exclaimed Jack. "That sloth is so cool!"

Zoe beamed with pride. Jack was right. But Sabina wasn't just cool – she was a hero. A real super sloth!

Zoe's Rescue Zoo

**Look out for MORE
amazing animal adventures
at the Rescue Zoo!**

The Secret Rescuers

If you enjoyed this book,
we think you'll love The Secret Rescuers!

Look out for another AMAZING series from Nosy Crow!